aarlibarnangg (seafood)

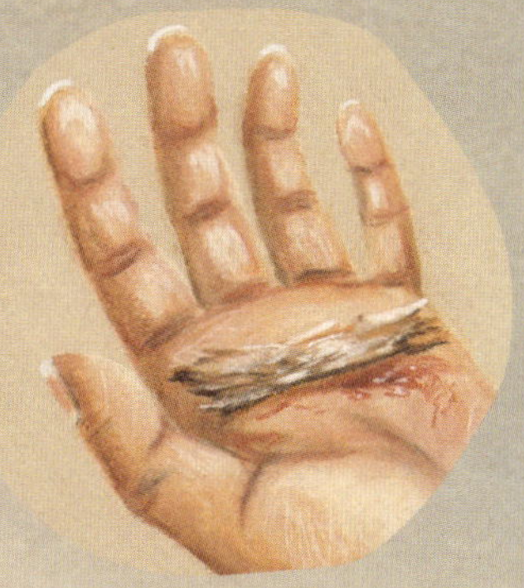

ganboor (paperbark tree)

gooljoo (spinifex grass)

biddin (waterholes)

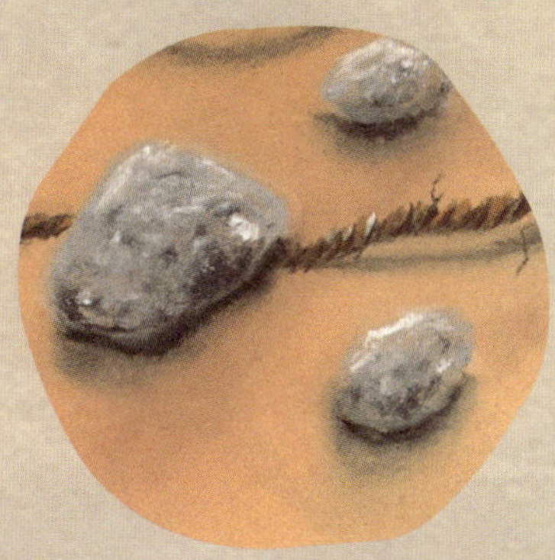

goolboo (stones)

gardin (rock shelters)

baali (large shelter)

lina (firesticks)

mayoorr (fish traps)

Published in 2024 by Hardie Grant Explore, an imprint of Hardie Grant Publishing

Hardie Grant Explore (Melbourne)
Wurundjeri Country
Building 1, 658 Church Street
Richmond, Victoria 3121

Hardie Grant Explore (Sydney)
Gadigal Country
Level 7, 45 Jones Street
Ultimo, NSW 2007

www.hardiegrant.com/au/explore

A catalogue record for this book is available from the National Library of Australia

Hardie Grant acknowledges the Traditional Owners of the Country on which we work, the Wurundjeri People of the Kulin Nation and the Gadigal People of the Eora Nation, and recognises their continuing connection to the land, waters and culture. We pay our respects to their Elders past and present.

Ask Aunty: Bush Survival Skills
ISBN 9781741179231

10 9 8 7 6 5 4 3 2 1

**Publisher**
Amanda Louey
**Project editor**
Amanda Louey
**Editor**
Kristina Schulz
**Proofreader**
Rema Gnanadickam
**Design and typesetting**
Jo Hunt
**Production manager**
Simone Wall

Colour reproduction by Splitting Image Colour Studio

Printed and bound in China by LEO Paper Products LTD.

The paper this book is printed on is certified against the Forest Stewardship Council® Standards and other sources. FSC® promotes environmentally responsible, socially beneficial and economically viable management of the world's forests.

# Bush Survival Skills

An introduction to First Nations bush survival skills

Aunty Munya Andrews

Illustrated by

Charmaine Ledden-Lewis

Hardie Grant
EXPLORE

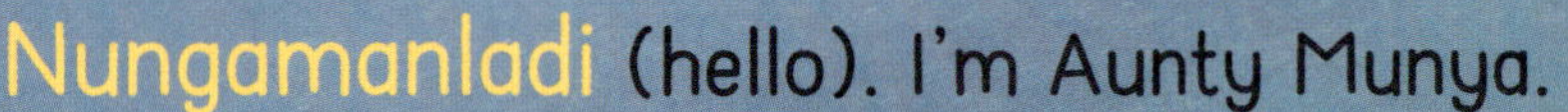

Nungamanladi (hello). I'm Aunty Munya.

I'm an Aboriginal Elder from Bardi Country, which is in the Kimberley in Western Australia.

We Bardi People live by the sea on Saltwater Country, so we call ourselves gaara ambooriny (Saltwater People).

Being an Elder doesn't mean I'm old (well, maybe just a little bit).

It means my responsibility is to teach others about my culture and my Country.

Did you know that for my people our land, our Country, is family, too? It is our connection to the Old People – the Ancestors – and to our identity.

That's why we must look after Country, the way you look after your kantrimin (family).

It was the spirit ancestors who first taught us things, including how to look after Country.

One of these spirit ancestors was Galaloong, who taught us our language and named all the places on Bardi Country.

He taught us our stories, our dances and our songs. He also taught us to not be greedy and to share what we have.

We owe everything to Galaloong.

Today, I want to talk to you about how booroo (Country) teaches us some incredible survival skills. This knowledge has been passed down through the generations by our Elders and families.

My people have been living on Country for tens of thousands of years. Like family, the bush looks after us – it feeds, shelters and comforts us.

If you were going camping in the bush,
what things would you take?

Definitely food and water, and maybe
something to make a fire with.

Oh, of course, don't forget
the tent for shelter.

Imagine what you would do if you were in the bush without all of these things.

This is where bush survival skills can help. The Elders taught us how to survive in the bush, while respecting it, by showing us how to find mayi (food) and oola (water), how to build shelter and how to make fire.

Let me tell you about surviving in the bush on Bardi Country.

# Finding water

We all need oola to survive – especially where my people live. Bardi Country is on a peninsula and is surrounded by saltwater on three sides – at the tip, to the west and to the east. There are no rivers or permanent surface waters apart from some small tidal creeks.

There are stories of people arriving on Bardi Country as strangers to the land. They try to find water, but they can't see it or it disappears on them, and they end up lost. As a stranger, you must be introduced to Country to be able to find water.

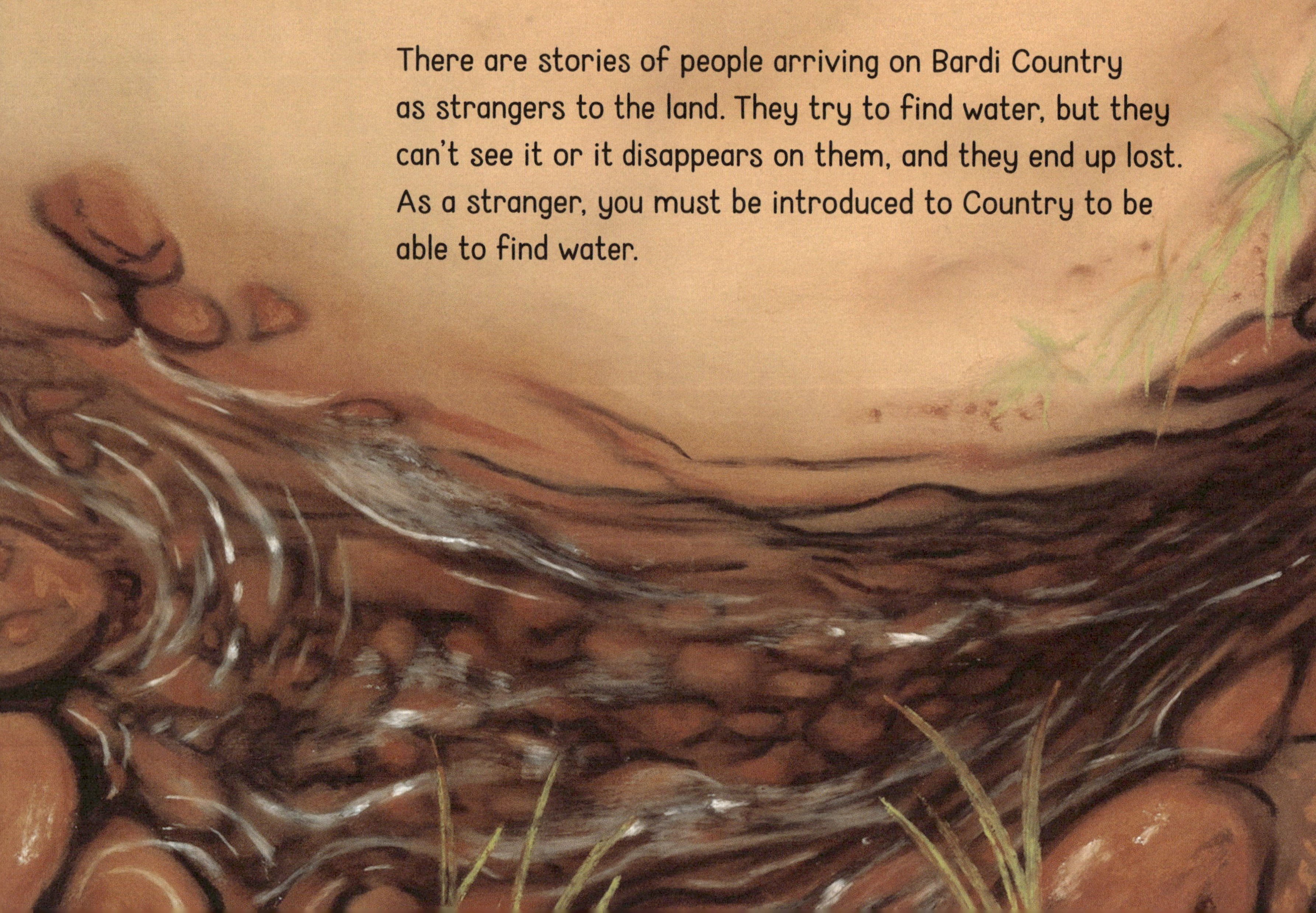

You can be introduced by an Elder or you can introduce yourself. Rub your armpit with your hand and place it in water so that Country can smell you and know you. If you do this, you will no longer be a stranger!

The other way is by speaking to Country. Say nungamanladi to the Old People, the spirits of the land, before stating your name, where you come from and your intentions on Country. Then, Country can be your best friend or family, too!

It's important that we know Country to understand where traditional water places are. Biddin (waterholes), oombarn (water soakages) and native wells are dotted around the coastline.

One way to find oombarn is by watching where birds and small animals go. We cover waterholes and native wells with paperbark and logs to prevent them from drying up or getting spoiled by animals.

There are many freshwater springs on Bardi Country. They can be hard to spot because they are covered with grass. Always be on the look out, and as you get close to them you need to be very careful not to fall in!

# Finding bush food and medicine

Aboriginal people know a lot about bush foods and medicinal plants, and often they're not just for eating.

Many foods can only be found in a particular season. You need to know the Bardi calendar to know what food is around, when it is available, and where to find it. Bardi Country has six seasons.

There are some foods that are available all year, like muunga (bush honey) and the boab nut.

Muunga is made by bush bees and is easy to find in trees and logs. It is also called 'sugarbag' because of the sac that contains the honey. Bush bees do not sting, which makes it safe to collect from the hives. Muunga is so sweet!

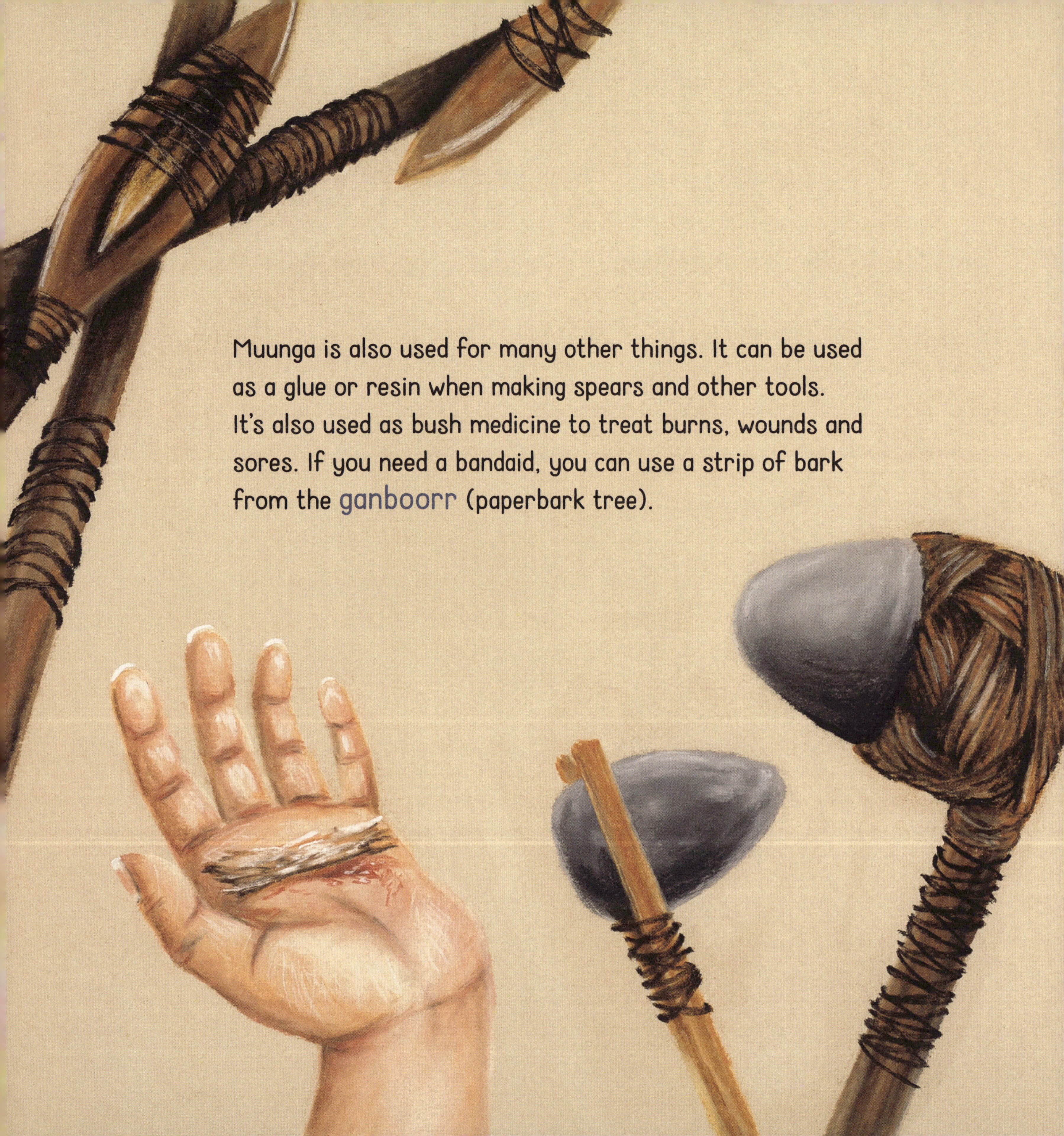

Muunga is also used for many other things. It can be used as a glue or resin when making spears and other tools. It's also used as bush medicine to treat burns, wounds and sores. If you need a bandaid, you can use a strip of bark from the ganboorr (paperbark tree).

Have you seen a boab nut before?
You may have seen a carved one like this.

The boab nut is wet and fleshy during the wet season (delicious!), but becomes chalky and paste-like during the dry season. When crushed, you can add water to the fruit surrounding the nut to make a cool, refreshing drink.

The tough nutshell can also be used as the perfect container to keep food fresh and make it easy to carry. It can also be used as a cup, to drink from.

Generally aarlibarnangg (seafood), vegetables and mayi (food) are more reliable than seasonal foods like fruits. As Saltwater People, a lot of our food comes from the ocean.

After eating, shells were left behind in a midden, a food rubbish pile away from the ocean. As children, we were told stories about the Goonboon, women spirits who are guardians of the mangroves and who made sure we looked after Country by only taking what we needed to survive. They were scary, so we always did the right thing!

# Tides

Did you know that the ocean waters of Bardi Country have one of the highest tides in the world?

Tides affect when we can fish and collect shellfish, so it's extremely important to know when the ocean's waters are rising and falling.

In my language, there are names for the many different tides. The tides are named based on their strength, their direction and the time of day.

The tide that arrives in the early morning is called bonan and the tide that goes out in the afternoon is called joombalmoorri.

When giving directions to others, Bardi People use the movement of the tides. They say joodarrarr (with the tide) or arrinarr (against the tide), instead of left or right.

## Finding places

If you are a stranger to our land, you can get lost because Country can change or conceal itself from you. But if Country knows who you are, then it will protect you and keep you safe.

Out on the open water, we follow the ocean's currents to help lead us where we need to go. We let animals, like dolphins or stingrays, guide the way.

## Fishing, hunting and trapping

Like other Saltwater People who live by the sea, Bardi People get much of their food from the ocean, so aril-ngan (fishing) is a way of life. But just like food on land, different fish are found at different times of the year.

Bardi hunting techniques include looking for signs that animals have been around, following their tracks, and setting up traps and using spears.

Bardi People make wirli-wirli (fishing lines) from fig-tree string. Ganji (shells) and goolboo (stones) are used as hooks and sinkers.

Besides fishing and spearing, Bardi People use mayoorr (fish traps) and fish poison, or both.

There are permanent fish traps in several areas on Bardi Country. Some are used for moonlight hunting at oondoog (night) where the fish come into the trap while garra (the tide) comes in. Before the tide turns, any gaps in the stones are plugged with gooljoo (spinifex grass).

Everyone works along the trap line, holding spinifex torches to make sure the fish don't escape as the tide goes out. The fish are collected when the water level drops.

Bardi People also cleverly discovered how to use two types of fish poison to help gather food. Both come from plant tubers and are not harmful to humans.

Using traps and poison to catch fish shows how Bardi People have been using science for tens of thousands of years.

## Building shelter

Aboriginal people have developed many clever shelter-building techniques using natural materials like bark, leaves and branches.

Simple lean-to windbreaks called loonggin and larger structures called baali were constructed from idool (pandanus) or other palms. People slept on the ground, mostly on the soft sand on the beach.

These shelters are still used on the beach, mostly for shade. They shelter us from the sun or from rain in the wet seasons.

You can also use gardin (rock shelters) to provide some shelter from the wind, sun or rain.

## Making fire

It takes skill to make a good fire without matches. Like other First Nations People, Bardi know how to make fire from scratch by rubbing two pieces of wood together to make a spark. We call these lina (firesticks). The spark catches on a pile of dry leaves or spinifex grass and sets them alight. The ashes and charcoal left behind are used for other things as well, including body paint and cave painting.

We need noord for light and warmth and to cook our food. Noord means many things to us, including the first spark of life and the warmth of family.

Fire is also used to make laalboo (earth ovens) where food is cooked in the ground. Anyjoo (yams) are always roasted in laalboo. Goonkoordoo (smoke) is also useful as an insect repellent, especially during Irallboo season, from April to May, when there are mosquitoes.

So, aamba-baawa oorany-baawa (boys and girls), what do you think?

I love my culture and I love my Country. But most of all,
I love sharing it with you.

# A note from Aunty Munya

Nungamanladi aamba-baawa oorany-baawa (hello, boys and girls)

You will have noticed that I have included many Bardi words in the text. The English words follow the Bardi words so that you know what each word means.

# A note about pronunciation

Aboriginal words sound very different from the way they are written using the English alphabet.

For example, the letters 'c' and 'k' sound like 'g' in my language.
So, Mankal (rainy season) is pronounced as Man**g**al.

The 'a' in Mankal sounds more like 'u' in the word 'up' rather than the 'a' in 'apple'. We say Mungal.

In most Aboriginal languages, stress is always placed on the first syllable of words. For example, Mankal is pronounced **Mung**-al.

# Other things to know

Like English, some Bardi words are compound words. For example, our word for rain, oola inarn, means water spear, which is so poetic.

Many Bardi words are collective. I have chosen these over single items. For example, the collective term for oyster and shellfish is barnangga, whereas Bardi distinguishes between different types of oysters and shellfish.

As in English, the same word can mean different things. For example, oonkoonkool means both ocean and storms. Booroo means Country as well as kangaroo, while lalin means season and year. Lalin also refers specifically to married turtle season, even though the Bardi word for married turtle is oondoord.

# Resources

If you would like to find out how to pronounce other words in the text, you can visit our website: evolves.com.au

# Author Acknowledgements

Big Esso to my Bardi Ancestors for giving me language and culture from which to view the world and to understand my place in it. Special thanks to Carla Rogers, my co-director, for her encouragement, support and guidance on this special journey.

Aunty Munya Andrews is an Elder from the Kimberley region of Western Australia. Educated in Australia and the USA, she has degrees in anthropology and law. She is the co-director of Evolve Communities Pty Ltd, which specialises in cultural awareness training, Reconciliation and Ally accreditation. Aunty is passionate about keeping Indigenous languages alive to leave behind a legacy for everyone.

What would you like to ask Aunty? I love your questions and learning together. You can contact me here:

admin@evolves.com.au.
@evolve.cultural.awareness
@evolvecommunities
@evolvecommunities
@evolvecommunities